Esther's Gragger

A Toyshop Tale of Purim

By Martha Seif Simpson

Illustrated by
D. Yael Bernhard

To all people, young and old,
who have the courage to stand up for justice
in the face of intolerance or cruelty

—MSS

For Dee,
an angel of Jewish learning

—DYB

Esther's Gragger: A Toyshop Tale of Purim. Text copyright © 2019 Martha Seif Simpson, Illustrations copyright © 2019 Durga Yael Bernhard. Wisdom Tales is an imprint of World Wisdom, Inc. All rights reserved. No part of this book may be used or reproduced in any manner without written permission, except in critical articles and reviews. Designed by Durga Yael Bernhard.

Library of Congress Cataloging-in-Publication Data
Names: Simpson, Martha Seif, 1954- author. | Bernhard, Durga Yael, illustrator.
Title: Esther's gragger : a toyshop tale of Purim / by Martha Seif Simpson;
illustrated by Durga Yael Bernhard.
Description: Bloomington, Indiana : Wisdom Tales, [2019] | Summary: A shopkeeper
who grumbles about the noise of Purim graggers uses one to chase away a mean boy who tries
to steal the special gragger Ben bought for his sister, Esther. |
Identifiers: LCCN 2018027552 (print) | LCCN 2018033840 (ebook) | ISBN
9781937786762 (epub) | ISBN 9781937786755 (casebound : alk. paper)
Subjects: | CYAC: Toys--Fiction. | Behavior--Fiction. | Purim--Fiction. | Toy stores--Fiction. | Jews--Fiction.
Classification: LCC PZ7.S6073 (ebook) | LCC PZ7.S6073 Est 2019 (print) | DDC [E]--dc23
LC record available at https://url.emailprotection.link/?aQIGj4lOvUgMGIEdjJ2U_yE_aZgYRcz_ttublcQn0bw4~

Printed in China on acid-free paper.
Production Date: August 2018
Plant & Location: Printed through Asia Pacific Offset
Job/Batch#: Q18080069
For information address Wisdom Tales,
P.O. Box 2682, Bloomington, Indiana, 47402-2682
www.wisdomtalespress.com

Raash! Raash! Raash!

The peddler swung his hands in circles to make the graggers turn. "Each one is unique and in perfect working order."

"Yes, I can tell!" groaned the shopkeeper. "That's the only thing I dislike about Purim. My customers always try the graggers and the sound gives me such a headache!"

He looked at the mysterious man in front of him. The peddler had come to sell him toys for his store.

The peddler chuckled as he turned to go. "I understand. But as the story teaches us, it takes a loud noise to drown out wickedness."

The graggers were indeed handsome. One showed the hero of the Purim story, Mordecai. Another portrayed lovely Esther, the brave queen who saved her people. Others displayed evil Haman, good King Ahasuerus, biblical scenes, or fanciful designs.

The shopkeeper arranged them next to the Purim masks.

Before long, a boy entered the shop.

"Good morning, sir," he said. "May I see your graggers?"

The shopkeeper pointed. "These arrived today."

The boy smiled. "They're all beautiful, but I like this one best."

"Queen Esther?"

"It's for my little sister. Her name is also Esther." He checked the price and pulled coins from his pockets. "Oh, no! I don't have enough. Could you hold this for me?"

The shopkeeper's grin faded. Most people who asked him to save an item never returned. "I'm sorry, but..."

"Please!" begged the boy. "My sister has been chosen to lead the Purim parade, and I want her to have a special gragger."

"Very well," the shopkeeper sighed. "I will hold it until eleven o'clock. If you don't come by then, I will put it out for sale again."

"Thank you!" called the boy as he left.

"We shall see," said the man.

A steady stream of customers visited the toyshop after the boy left. And everyone played with the graggers, whether they wanted to buy one or not.

"Oy, what a noise!" the shopkeeper moaned. "I will be glad when they are all sold."

As eleven o'clock approached, a tall boy banged the door open and strode into the shop.

"Where are your noisemakers?" he shouted. Then he saw the Esther gragger on the shelf. "Give me that fancy one!" he demanded.

"I'm sorry, but that gragger is being held for another customer," replied the shopkeeper, trying to keep his patience. "But I have a few others that..."

"I'll pay you double for it," interrupted the boy.

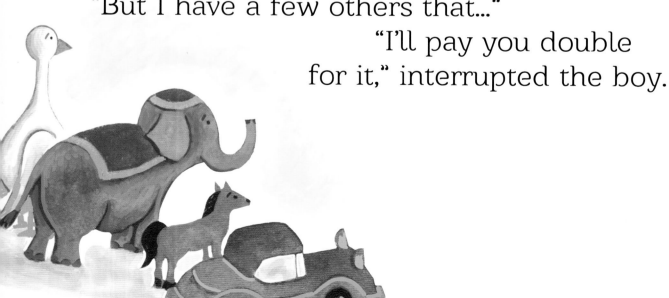

The shopkeeper glanced at his watch. It was nearly eleven o'clock and he had a chance to make twice as much money. Should he sell it now or honor his agreement to wait?

"Come on, come on!" The boy slapped the counter. "Just sell it to me!"

The shopkeeper made his decision. "I don't do business with rude people," he replied in a firm voice. "Please take your money and leave my shop."

The boy mumbled a curse and left, slamming the door.

A minute later, the boy from that morning rushed in with a young girl. They were both wearing costumes. She was dressed as Queen Esther.

"Here we are," he said, slightly out of breath. "We ran the whole way. Do you still have the gragger?"

"I do." The shopkeeper placed it in the girl's hands. "You must be Esther. Your brother chose this especially for you."

"Oh, it's perfect!" Esther exclaimed. She rewarded him with a smile bright enough to chase away the annoyances of his morning. Then she hugged her brother. "Thank you so much, Ben!"

"And thank you," he said, paying the shopkeeper. "*Chag Sameach* – Happy Purim!"

"And to you." The shopkeeper waved goodbye.

But as the children crossed the street, the tall boy blocked their way. "So the old man was saving that noisemaker for you! Too bad you won't get to keep it."

He tried to snatch it from the girl, but she held on tightly. "My name is Esther," she cried. "And I'm not scared of mean people!"

"We don't want any trouble," Ben told the boy. "Please just leave us alone."

The tall boy let go of the gragger and pushed Ben aside. "Not until I get what I want!" he yelled.

The shopkeeper heard all the shouting and looked out his window.

Esther was not backing down. Instead, she held up her gragger and whirled it. This surprised the tall boy, who stepped back. "Put that down!" he demanded.

The shopkeeper knew what to do. He took two of the unsold noisemakers and hurried outside. Keeping one, he handed

the other to Ben. They spun their graggers along with Esther.

Raash! Raash! Raash! The racket echoed throughout the town square, getting louder and louder. People stopped to look at the commotion. Some had graggers of their own, and began to spin them.

The tall boy covered his ears to shut out the deafening noise. "Stop!" he cried.

The shopkeeper silenced his gragger, as did the others. "Meanness is not welcome here," he announced. "Leave now, and never bother these children again!" The crowd joined in, calling to the boy to leave.

Ashamed, the boy hurried away without another word.

"Thank you!" exclaimed Esther and Ben at once to the shopkeeper.

The shopkeeper nodded. "And thank you, my dear, for reminding us all what Purim is really about. Costumes are pretty and festivals are fun, but we must never be afraid to take a stand against cruelty. You, young Esther, have the spirit of your namesake. You will make a fine leader for the Purim parade."

"And I have just the right gragger to do it!" said Esther with a smile. Then she and her brother said goodbye and joined a parade of children marching toward the synagogue.

As the shopkeeper watched the parade pass, he saw the peddler was watching too. The peddler waved, and the shopkeeper waved back.

"I think, my friend,
I shall never again
complain about the sound
of graggers!"

What is Purim?

Purim (pronounced *poo'rim*) is a joyous holiday that usually comes in March, or sometimes late February. On the Jewish calendar (which has lunar months), it is the 14th day of Adar. Purim celebrates the time when a brave young queen named Esther saved the lives of the Jewish people living in ancient Persia. Esther's cousin, Mordecai, refused to bow down to Haman, the cruel advisor to the king. So Haman plotted to destroy all the Jews in the kingdom. When Esther told King Ahasuerus about Haman's plan, the good king agreed to protect the Jews and punished wicked Haman instead. King Ahasuerus had not known that Esther was Jewish, so it took a great deal of courage for her to admit this to him and ask for his help. Esther could have easily kept her secret and turned her back on her people. But she chose instead to risk her life and do the right thing. That was very brave, indeed!

Mordecai

Queen Esther King Ahasuerus

Haman

Purim Practices Today

Modern-day Jews celebrate Purim by going to synagogue to read the Book of Esther, called the *Megillah*; by creating a comical play about the story of Esther, called a *Purimshpiel*; and, especially fun for children, by dressing up in festive costumes to take part in a Purim parade or carnival. During the reading of the *Megillah*, people shout, stamp their feet, and use their graggers to make as much noise as they can whenever Haman's name is mentioned. This follows an ancient custom to blot out the name of an enemy with noise in order to stamp out evil. Thus, Purim is a wonderful time to talk to children about upholding their rights and fighting against injustice. In our story, Esther stands up to the mean boy and uses the noise of the graggers to make him back down.

Another custom is for people to send gifts of food or drink to friends, family, and those in need. This practice is called *shalach manos* in Yiddish, *mishloach manot* in Hebrew (meaning the "sending of portions"), and is part of a charitable tradition called *tzedakah*. A special treat included in many Purim baskets are the triangular fruit-filled cookies called *hamentaschen*, which are supposed to represent Haman's three-cornered hat. In our story, Esther has been chosen to lead the Purim parade as a reward for her efforts at *shalach manos*.

What are Graggers?

The English word "gragger" (usually pronounced *greh'gr* or *grah'gr*) comes from the Yiddish word for a noisemaker or rattle. There are many types of graggers, but the one used by Esther, Ben, and the shopkeeper is a ratchet device made of wood. A ratchet has a gearwheel and a strong "tongue" that is mounted on a handle. When you swing the handle in a circular motion, the tongue clicks against the gearwheel, making a rattling noise that sounds like *Raash! Raash! Raash!* And "ra'ash" (רעש) just happens to be the Hebrew word for "noise." The faster you spin the gragger, the louder the noise it makes. Today, many of the ratchet-type graggers are made of lightweight tin or plastic.

There are other types of noisemakers you can use at Purim, including shakers and tambourines.

Make Your Own Noisemakers

To make a shaker, you can use a clean tin can, yogurt cup, frozen juice container, small milk carton, or other container of a similar size. Fill the container about 1/4 full with small bells, pebbles, dried beans, or rice. Cover the container and seal it well with masking tape. Decorate it by covering the outside with wrapping paper, stickers, or pictures you have drawn. Then, hold it tight and shake away!

If you prefer to make a tambourine, get two stiff paper plates. Decorate the bottoms any way you like. Put one plate on top of the other so the decorated sides face outward. Staple the edges of the plates together about half way around. Drop small bells, pebbles, dried beans, or rice inside so it's half full. Finish stapling the edges together and put masking tape around the edges to cover the staples. Have fun making noise with your tambourine!

Make a few shakers and tambourines using different containers and fillings to compare how they sound.

Chag Purim Sameach –
(khahg poo'rim sa-may'akh)
Happy Purim!

About the Author & Illustrator

MARTHA SEIF SIMPSON is an author and children's librarian, currently in her twenty-fifth year as head of children's services at the Stratford Library in Stratford, CT. She is the author of five professional books for teachers and librarians as well as two children's books: *What NOT to Give Your Mom on Mother's Day* and *The Dreidel That Wouldn't Spin: A Toyshop Tale of Hanukkah*. Martha enjoyed celebrating Hanukkah and Purim with her parents and brother while growing up, and sharing these customs with her own children and husband. She lives in Hamden, CT. Martha's website can be found at martha-seif-simpson.com.

DURGA YAEL BERNHARD is the illustrator, designer, and author of numerous award-winning children's books. She brings a variety of influences to her work, including African art; studies in Eastern and Western religion; and a love of nature that fills her daily life in the Catskill Mountains of NY where she makes her home. Ms. Bernhard is also a fine-art painter, an arts-in-ed teacher, and a bnei mitzvah tutor. Her titles include *Never Say a Mean Word Again* and *The Dreidel That Wouldn't Spin*. Visit her blog and website at dyaelbernhard.com.